The Three Billygoats Gruff
and Mean Calypso Joe

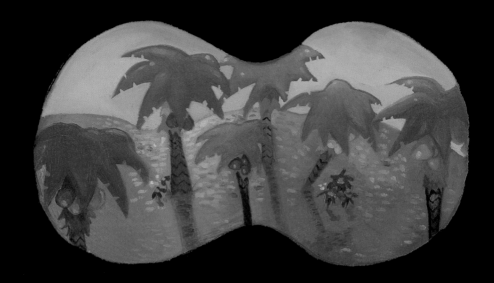

To Anna, Phil, and Greg

—C. V. Y.

To my family

—K. S.

Atheneum Books for Young Readers

An imprint of Simon & Schuster Children's Publishing Division

1230 Avenue of the Americas

New York, New York 10020

Book design Abelardo Martínez

The text of this book is set in Cantoria.

The illustrations are rendered in acrylic.

Printed in Hong Kong

10 9 8 7 6 5 4 3 2

Library of Congress Cataloging-in-Publication Data

Youngquist, Cathrene Valente.

Three Billygoats Gruff and Mean Calypso Joe / written by Cathrene

Valente Youngquist ; illustrated by Kristin Sorra.—1st ed.

p. cm.

Summary: In this retelling of the Norwegian tale, three clever billy goats

outwit Calypso Joe, a big ugly troll that lives under the bridge

on Split in Two Island in the Caribbean Sea.

ISBN 0-689-82824-1

[1. Fairy tales. 2. Folklore—Norway.] I. Title: Three billygoats Gruff.

II. Sorra, Kristin, ill. III. Asbjornsen, Peter Christen, 1812–1885.

Tre bukkene Bruse. IV. Title.

PZ8.Y89 Th 2001

[398.2]—dc21

[E]   00-040153

The Three Billygoats Gruff
and Mean Calypso Joe

Written by **Cathrene Valente Youngquist**

Illustrated by **Kristin Sorra**

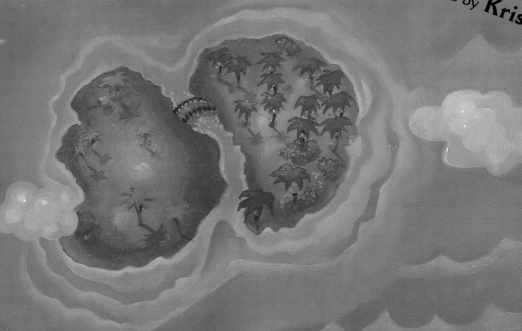

Atheneum Books for Young Readers
New York   London   Toronto   Sydney   Singapore

There once were three billygoats of the family Gruff: Little Billygoat, Williegoat, and Captain Bill E. Goat. They lived quite happily on Split in Two Island, floating in the sparkling Caribbean Sea.

Split in Two was a most unusual island,
for here the Atlantic Ocean cut through
to the Caribbean Sea,

and the only way to get from one side of the
island to the other was to cross a bridge guarded
by a cranky old troll, Calypso Joe.

Calypso Joe lived under the bridge in the craggy rocks.
He was the meanest troll on that part of the island, with
eyes big as coconuts, seaweed hair flying. Whenever anyone
would try to cross his bridge, he would roar,

"I am Calypso Joe,
   de meanest troll dis part of de island.
   Nobody cross dis bridge, but first he pay de toll!"

For many years the three Billygoats Gruff were quite content on their side of the island. But then they began to yearn for that other side, lush and green, set about with tropical delights and delectable goat treats.

The littlest billygoat was the first to start across the bridge. *Trip-trop, trippety-trop, trip-trop,* his hoofbeats echoed under the bridge and through the craggy rocks.

"Hey, man!" roared Calypso Joe.
"Who's dat crossin' me bridge?
Makin' all de racket, distuhbin' me sleep!"

"It is I, Little Billygoat Gruff," said the littlest billygoat.
"I am goin' ovah for some-ting to eat."

"Big problem!" roared the troll, eyes big as coconuts, seaweed hair flying.

"I am Calypso Joe,
    de meanest troll dis part of de island.
    Nobody cross dis bridge, but first he pay de toll!"

"I don't have any-ting, Mistah Troll," said the little billygoat. "Please let me go now. I am so-o hungry!"

"Well, so's dis troll, and I eat good goat in one mouthful," growled mean Calypso Joe.

"Oh, Mistah Troll, you don't want me," said the littlest billygoat in his little billygoat voice. "Me mama says I am de runt of de family and if I don't eat I will blow right away. Me big brother, he is comin' and he's a betta' mouthful. You try him."

"Okay, goat," grumped mean Calypso Joe. "No problem. You go."

Over the bridge went the littlest Billygoat Gruff, *trip-trop, trippety-trop, trip-trop.*

The next goat to start across the bridge was the middle-sized goat. *Clip-clop, clippety-clop, clip-clop,* his hoofbeats echoed under the bridge and through the craggy rocks.

"Hey, man!" roared Calypso Joe. "Who's dat crossin' me bridge? Makin' all de racket, distuhbin' me sleep!"

"Just me, Williegoat Gruff, headin' ovah for some bite to eat," said the middle-sized goat.

"Big problem!" roared the troll,
eyes big as coconuts, seaweed
hair flying.

"I am Calypso Joe,
de meanest troll dis part of de island.
Nobody cross dis bridge,
but first he pay de toll!"

"Sorry, troll, I am all out," said Williegoat. "Just let me go an' I catch you next time. I am very hungry today!"

"Well, so's dis troll, and I eat good goat in one mouthful," growled mean Calypso Joe.

"Oh, you don't want me," said Williegoat in his medium-goat voice. "I am all bones inside, and dey'll stick in your throat. Me big brother, he is comin' and he's just your mouthful. You try him."

"Okay, goat," grumped mean Calypso Joe. "No problem. You go."

Over the bridge went Williegoat Gruff, *clip-clop, clippety-clop, clip-clop.*

The last goat to start across the bridge was Captain
Bill E. Goat Gruff, a giant of a billygoat. His massive horns
hung low to the ground. *Crump-grumph, crump-de-grumph,
crump-grumph,* his hoofbeats thundered under the bridge
and through the craggy rocks.

"Hey, man!" roared Calypso Joe.
"Who's dat crossin' me bridge?
Makin' all de racket, distuhbin' me sleep!"

"It is I, Captain Bill E. Goat Gruff," answered the biggest billygoat of all.

"Big problem!" roared the troll, eyes big as coconuts, seaweed hair flying.

"I am Calypso Joe,
   de meanest troll dis part of de island.
   Nobody cross dis bridge, but first he pay de toll!"

"I have got nothin' for you, troll," said the biggest Billygoat Gruff. "I am goin' 'cross dis bridge, for I AM VERY HUNGRY!"

"Well, so's dis troll, and I eat good goat in one mouthful," growled mean Calypso Joe. He leaped one great leap onto the bridge and gave his fiercest troll glare.

Captain Bill E. Goat glared right back. Then, in a rumbly voice, he said, "You don't want dis goat, 'cause I am gonna 'Grumph' you right off de bridge. And you, troll. You gotta learn some manners!"

Then that giant of a billygoat lowered his horns, gave one last glare, and he charged, *crump-grumph, crump-de-grumph, crump-grumph.* His hoofbeats thundered through the bridge and just about shattered the craggy rocks.

Ka-Grumphphph! He butted that troll right into the water.
Ker-splashshsh! There lay mean Calypso Joe, just as
stunned as he could be.

Captain Bill E. Goat Gruff
then went on across the bridge,
*crump-grumph, crump-de-grumph,
crump-grumph,* where he joined
his brothers for lunch in the
lush, green garden beyond.

The three Billygoats Gruff
stuffed themselves until they
were exactly filled to the horns
and about ready to burst.

When they headed back to the bridge, there was Calypso
Joe, all washed up, his seaweed hair plastered behind his
ears, and . . . he had found himself some manners.

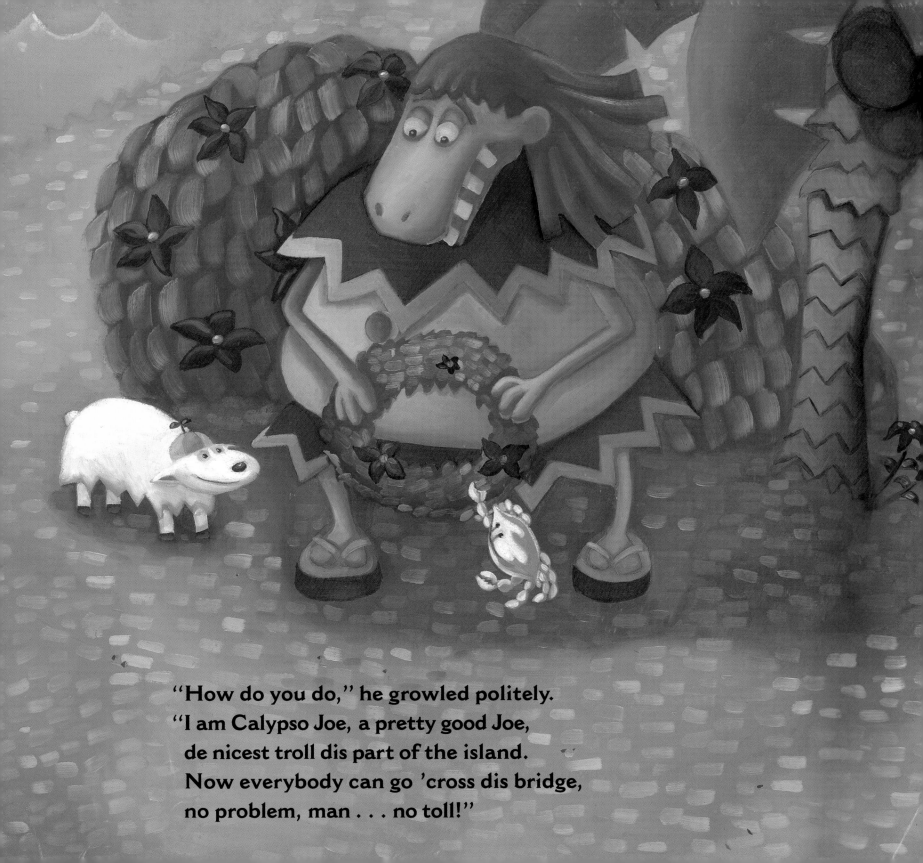

"How do you do," he growled politely.
"I am Calypso Joe, a pretty good Joe,
de nicest troll dis part of the island.
Now everybody can go 'cross dis bridge,
no problem, man . . . no toll!"

Calypso Joe from then on remained a pretty good Joe.
That is, most of the time. Being a troll, of course, he would
sometimes forget his manners, and then the seaweed flew. But
no problem. The goats would bump him back into the ocean
for a sea bath, and then everything was once again okay.